For Alexander and Georgia May   H.M.

For Katherine and Judith   N.J.

With thanks to farmer Richard Aldous
for his technical assistance

First published 1987 by
Walker Books Ltd
184-192 Drummond Street
London NW1 3HP

First printed 1987
Printed and bound by L.E.G.O., Vicenza, Italy

British Library Cataloguing in Publication Data
Maisner, Heather
Kate and the cutter.—(The Tractors of Thomson's Yard)
I. Title II. Johnson, Norman III. Series
823'.914 [J]   PZ7

ISBN 0-7445-0419-8

KATE
AND THE CUTTER

WRITTEN BY

HEATHER MAISNER

ILLUSTRATED BY

NORMAN JOHNSON

WALKER BOOKS
LONDON

"I'm Kate, Kate, usually late . . ."

Tractor Kate mumbled the first line of her song, half opened her eyes, took a quick look at the cold February morning and closed them again. She was soon asleep once more, the hedge-cutting machine resting heavily against her.

A few moments later she was woken by the voice of the neighbour's tractor, Len. He was hurrying along the main road with his hedge-cutting machine tucked in beside him, shouting, "I've only one hedge left to do! I'll finish before you!"

"Come on, Kate. Hurry up." The tractors and animals crowded round. "We know you can beat Len."

Every year there was a race to see who would finish cutting the hedges first. Kate had been trimming hedges every day for two months. She had only one hedge left to do.

"I'll finish before you!" shouted Len.

Rosemary, the farmer's daughter, climbed into the driving seat and started the engine, but Kate groaned, "I can't go on. I'm stiff all over and I've got a headache." Her engine spluttered and stopped.

The animals and tractors frowned. "It's all right," said tractor Jack. "All you need is some more diesel." Rosemary restarted the engine, drove Kate to the pump and filled her tank. Then they set off down the drive.

Halfway to the gate Kate coughed and cried, "Help! My clutch has gone! I know my clutch has gone." She rolled her eyes and stopped.

"You've probably just stalled," said tractor Jack. "Your engine's still cold. Relax and you'll be all right."

Rosemary turned the starter. The engine sprang into life and they set off smoothly again.

Kate rolled her eyes and stopped.

As they drove through the gate, Kate rocked slightly from side to side. "I've got a puncture," she wailed. "I know I've got a puncture." Immediately she stopped and Rosemary jumped down from the driving seat.

The animals and tractors strained forward to see. If Kate had a puncture, she wouldn't be able to work. It might take all day for the tyre servicemen to arrive. Loud-mouth Len would finish first. Rosemary checked Kate's tyres, back and front, but she couldn't find a puncture. At last they turned out of the yard.

"Come on, Kate, we know you can do it!" the animals and tractors shouted behind her.

"I've got a puncture," Kate wailed.

Puffing and blowing, but pulling herself together, Kate moved down the road. She went past the fields of wheat and oil-seed rape, round the pond and by the forest. In the distance she saw Farmer Thomson keeping pigeons off the rape with his gun. And everywhere she saw one neat hedge after another.

Slowly and steadily she climbed the hill. There before her stretched the last untrimmed hedge on the farm. On the other side of the road, his engine revving and his cutter whirling, was the neighbour's tractor, Len.

"Just got up, did you, Kate?" he laughed. "Getting a bit old for hedge-cutting, aren't you?" He carelessly flung some twigs across the road.

Len revved his engine and laughed.

Kate ignored him. She raised the ram of her cutter and started to trim. It was hard, heavy, monotonous work. She moved at one mile an hour, revving her engine, getting hotter and hotter. The traffic hooted around her. She avoided barbed wire under the branches and steered clear of flints and broken glass. The cutter rattled and Len shouted insults.

To drown out some of the noise, Kate started to sing:

"I'm Kate, Kate, usually late –"

"You can say that again," Len interrupted. "You're so late with this hedge, you might as well just give up."

"Nobody tells me when to give up!" shouted Kate.

She gritted her teeth, raised her cutting ram and went to work furiously. Soon she had trimmed almost as much of her hedge as Len had his. Nothing and nobody could stop her.

The traffic hooted around her.

But she hadn't seen the tiny rabbit caught in the hedge, looking up and too frightened even to cry out. Kate's eyes were fixed on a dangerous stretch of barbed-wire fencing. The cutter came closer and closer and closer. Soon it would cut the rabbit in two.

Kate glanced down and her eyes met the terrified eyes of the rabbit. What could she do to save it?

She swerved and swung the cutter against the hedge, closing the flails hard on the barbed wire. With a grinding sound and burning smell the wire spun and the cutters stopped dead. So did Kate.

"Really, Kate," laughed Len. "I thought you'd know better than that." He sent a broken bottle spinning across the road.

Her eyes met the terrified eyes of the rabbit.

Kate ignored Len. She was watching the rabbit. For a moment it hesitated. Then it darted out from the hedgerow, crashed into the broken bottle, sending it skidding towards Len, and hopped through the opposite hedge. Kate breathed a sigh of relief.

Len rocked with laughter as he watched Rosemary untangle the wire.

"What a joke! What a joke!" He laughed until tears came to his eyes. "See you later, Kate, if you ever get started again, that is." He revved up fiercely and drove straight onto the sharp point of the broken bottle. With a hiss the air started to go out of his tyre.

"Really, Len, I'm surprised," Kate smiled. "You've got a puncture. I thought you'd know better than that."

Len drove straight onto the broken bottle.

Rosemary finally freed the wire from the cutter and Kate set to work again. Soon she'd finished the last hedge on the farm. The Thomson tractors had won.

"Better luck next time!" she called to Len, who was still waiting helplessly for the tyre servicemen to arrive.

Kate tucked the cutting machine in beside her and headed back to the yard, passing one neat hedge after another and proudly singing her song:

"I'm Kate, Kate, usually late,
When things can be put off, I'll let them wait.
If I had my way,
I'd sleep all the day,
But no one can say I don't pull my weight!"

꧁ *Kate headed back to the yard, singing her song.* ꧂